CW01513235

Before reading

Look at the book cove
Ask, "What do you thir

To build independence
at the start of this book. If the child needs extra practice, turn
back to pages 6 and 7 in 3a and read the words again with
the child.

During reading

Offer plenty of support and praise as the child reads the story.
Listen carefully and respond to events in the text.

In 3c, the new **Key Words** are not shown at the bottom of
the page. If the child hesitates over a word, turn to the back
of the book to practise reading it together. If the word is
phonically decodable, you can sound out the letters and
blend the sounds to read the word ("d-o-g, dog"). Praise the
child for their effort, then return to the story.

Pause every few pages and ask questions to check the child's
understanding of what they have read. If they begin to lose
concentration, stop reading and save the page for later.

Celebrate the child's achievement and come back to the
story the next day.

After reading

After reading this book, ask, "Did you enjoy the story? What did
you like about it?" Encourage the child to share their opinions.

Use the comprehension questions on page 54 to check the
child's understanding and recall of the text.

Ladybird

Series Consultant: Professor David Waugh
With thanks to Kulwinder Maude

LADYBIRD BOOKS

UK | USA | Canada | Ireland | Australia
India | New Zealand | South Africa

Ladybird Books is part of the Penguin Random House group of companies
whose addresses can be found at global.penguinrandomhouse.com.
www.penguin.co.uk   www.puffin.co.uk   www.ladybird.co.uk

Penguin
Random House
UK

Original edition of Key Words with Peter and Jane first published by Ladybird Books Ltd 1964
Series updated 2023
This book first published 2023
001

Text copyright © Ladybird Books Ltd, 1964, 2023
Illustrations by Nuno Alexandre Vieira, Flora Aranyi, and Fran and David Brylewski
Based on characters and design by Gustavo Mazali
Illustrations copyright © Ladybird Books Ltd, 2023

With thanks to Liz Pemberton for her contributions in advising on the illustrations
With thanks to Inclusive Minds for connecting us with their Inclusion Ambassador network,
and in particular thanks to Guntaas Kaur Chugh for her input on the illustrations

Printed in China

The authorized representative in the EEA is Penguin Random House Ireland,
Morrison Chambers, 32 Nassau Street, Dublin D02 YH68

A CIP catalogue record for this book is available from the British Library

ISBN: 978-0-241-51081-0

All correspondence to:
Ladybird Books
Penguin Random House Children's
One Embassy Gardens, 8 Viaduct Gardens, London SW11 7BW

MIX
Paper from
responsible sources
FSC® C018179
FSC
www.fsc.org

Key Words

with Peter and Jane

3c

Peter and Jane's rabbits

Based on the original
Key Words with Peter and Jane
reading scheme and research by William Murray

Original edition written by William Murray
This edition written by Chitra Soundar
Illustrated by Nuno Alexandre Vieira, Flora Aranyi,
and Fran and David Brylewski
Based on characters and design by Gustavo Mazali

Peter and Jane go
to Will and Amber's
home to play.

Will and Amber
have rabbits.

"We can play with this rabbit," says Will.

"We can play with that rabbit," says Amber.

Peter and Jane
go home.

"Sameer!" says Jane.

"We played with
rabbits," says Peter.

"We like playing with Will and Amber's rabbits," Jane says to Mum.

"Can we get pet rabbits, Dad? Please, please, please!" says Peter.

"Yes, we can!" Dad says.

"We can go to that pet shop to get a home for the rabbits," says Dad.

They go into the
pet shop.

"This shop has
homes for rabbits,"
says Peter.

"Look at this rabbit home," Jane says.

"Please can we get that?" says Peter.

"Yes, we can," says Dad.

"Please can we get this shell for the rabbits?" says Peter.

"No, we can get that ball," says Mum.

"This is for the rabbits' water," says Jane.

"The rabbits can jump on this," says Dad.

Mum and Peter go into this shop.

"Please get that for the rabbits, Peter," Mum says.

The home for the rabbits goes into the car.

"Can this fit in?" says Jane.

Dad has fun with the rabbit home.

"This bit goes here," he says.

"Can this bit fit here?" Jane says.

"No. That bit goes in here," says Mum.

"Please can you get that box?" says Dad.

Peter says he can.

"We can fill this with water," Dad says.

"That box is for the hay," Mum says.

"And we have this
for the rabbits
to play with,"
says Jane.

"We have a rabbit home! Can we go and get the rabbits?" says Peter.

"Yes!" says Dad.

"We can get rabbits here. They have no homes," says Mum.

"This rabbit and that rabbit want homes," Dad says.

Peter and Jane like the rabbits.

"We can get the rabbits into the car and go home," says Dad.

The rabbits go
and look at the
rabbit home.

This rabbit gets the hay.

That rabbit gets into the home.

"You have rabbits!" Will says.

"Yes! Come and play!" says Peter.

Questions

Answer these questions about
the story.

1 Whose rabbits do Peter and Jane
   play with at the start of the story?

2 Where do Peter and Jane get a
   rabbit home?

3 How many rabbits do Peter and
   Jane get?

4 What do the rabbits do in their
   new home?